For children of all ages
who find peace in their hearts

Margaret K. McElderry Books
An imprint of Simon & Schuster Children's Publishing Division
1230 Avenue of the Americas, New York, New York 10020
Copyright © 2008 by Demi
Book design by Michael Nelson
The text for this book is set in Weiss.
The illustrations for this book are rendered in traditional Chinese paints and inks with pen and brush on vellum and watercolor paper.
Title calligraphy by Jeanyee Wong
Manufactured in China
2 4 6 8 10 9 7 5 3 1
LIBRARY OF CONGRESS CATALOGING-IN-PUBLICATION DATA
Demi.   The magic pillow / written and illustrated by Demi.—1st ed.   p. cm.
Summary: A poor young boy in China yearns for wealth and power, until a magician gives him a magic pillow
that brings dreams of what would happen if his wishes came true.
ISBN-13: 978-1-4169-2470-8   ISBN-10: 1-4169-2470-1 (hardcover)
[1. Contentment—Fiction. 2. Dreams—Fiction. 3. Magic—Fiction. 4. China—Fiction.] I. Title.
PZ7.D3925Mag 2008   E—dc22   2006029213

FIRST
EDITION

THE MAGIC PILLOW

WRITTEN

AND ILLUSTRATED BY

DEMI

MARGARET K. McELDERRY BOOKS
NEW YORK LONDON TORONTO SYDNEY

ONCE UPON A TIME IN CHINA
there was a boy named Ping.
His family owned a poor little patch of land,
but they were all very happy together.
Ping had a little black pony.
He liked to help out wherever he could.

One winter day
Ping rode into the mountains to collect firewood.
It began to snow so heavily and deeply
that Ping suddenly realized
he couldn't get home.

Not far away Ping could see the light of an inn.
He rode over to ask if he might stay there
till the storm stopped.

The innkeeper was a kind old man,
who invited Ping to come in
and have some noodle soup
that he was cooking.

A great magician was staying at the inn,
and he was performing magic tricks!
Ping could not believe his eyes!
Out of the magician's pocket
flew a dragon that circled round
the room—then disappeared
into his pocket again.

Next the great magician
dropped a tiny seed
into a vase.
It quickly grew
into a tree of diamonds,
radiating jewels of light
that landed right in
Ping's hands!

Ping closed his hands,
trying to hold on to the jewels,
but they vanished away.

Ping was so amazed that he could hardly speak.
How wonderful were the jewels of light!
But suddenly he remembered his family's poverty
and became very sad.

The great magician understood
Ping's feelings and sat down beside him.
"Tell me why you are so sad."

Ping replied, "It seems that in life
a person should do great things:
He should have money, power, fame,
and everything life can offer.

"But my family is so poor.
All I have is my little black pony,
and I don't think
I'll ever have any more."

"The greatest gift of all,"
said the great magician, "is having wisdom,
for with wisdom you can find the Truth!
You can become enlightened!
Here is a magic pillow.
Go to sleep on this pillow
and all your wishes
will come true!"

The pillow was smooth, and it just fit
Ping's neck and shoulders.
He was so tired that as soon as he lay down
and put his head on the pillow,
he went right to sleep.

Ping began to dream!
In his dream he was growing up
and he had hundreds of little black ponies!
He was marrying the most beautiful daughter
of the richest family, and he was living
in the grandest palace!

He was becoming famous!
He was an officer, then a high officer,
and then the highest officer!

Then he was commanding the largest army
and defeating the fiercest enemy!
He was being made prime minister of all the land!
He was being decorated with honors
and heaped with gifts!
He was powerful
and he was happy!

But then something was going wrong.
People were getting jealous of him.
They were telling lies and accusing him,
and he was being put in jail.

After a long, long time Ping was freed.

Ping was being made prime minister again!

And he was decorated with honors
and heaped with gifts!

All of his sons and grandsons were wanting money, power, and fame too.
Quickly they were marrying the most beautiful daughters of the richest families,

and quickly they were rising to power.

Quickly they conquered the fiercest enemy.

Quickly they were envied, accused, jailed, and pardoned, then reappointed high officers!

Ping was seeing the family fortunes rise and fall and rise and fall, like endless waves upon the ocean.

Money was like a flash of lightning in a summer cloud, power was like a flickering lamp, and fame lasted no longer than a bubble in a stream.

Ping was growing very old.
He was 108, and he had a
long white beard that reached
down to his feet.

At this point the little boy Ping
suddenly woke up.

It was morning.
The snow had stopped,
and the sun was shining.
He was still at the inn,
the great magician was
still performing magic tricks,
and the innkeeper was
still cooking noodle soup.
"Thank you, kind sir,
for letting me use your
magic pillow," Ping said.

"It is a wonderful gift indeed, and it has given me great wisdom. Now I know what it would be like to be a great man and have money, power, and fame. And now I know that I am happy just the way I am!"

With that he said
good-bye to the magician
and to the innkeeper,
and he rode home on his little black pony,
and he was singing all the way.

He who finds peace in his heart has found his palace of gold.

THE MAGIC PILLOW
is based on a Chinese short story
by Shen Jiji of the Tang Dynasty (700 A.D.).
The story takes place at a famous inn of Handan, a city in the Hebei province.
Lu Weng, a Taoist priest, was the great magician
who enlightened Tung Pin with a dream
about the vanity and illusion of all material wealth.
Tung Pin became one of the Eight Chinese Immortals (Lu),
thus known as Lu Tung Pin.
He is always depicted carrying a sword
to destroy greed, ego, passion, jealousy, and ignorance.
Also, Lu Tung Pin is the Patron Saint of Literature.

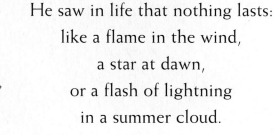

He saw in life that nothing lasts:
like a flame in the wind,
a star at dawn,
or a flash of lightning
in a summer cloud.

But within life
Heaven can be found,
and within Heaven
is life without end.